The Sheep that Saved CHRISTMAS

A Eweltide Tale

Written by Jason Page

Illustrated by Adrian Reynolds

RED FOX

For my mum - who loves Christmas
just as much as Cynthia! J.P.

For Matt and Kez A.R.

THE SHEEP THAT SAVED CHRISTMAS: A EWELTIDE TALE
A RED FOX BOOK 978 1 782 95590 0

Published in Great Britain by Red Fox,
an imprint of Random House Children's Publishers UK
A Random House Group Company
This edition published 2014
3 5 7 9 10 8 6 4 2
Text copyright © Jason Page, 2014
Illustrations copyright © Adrian Reynolds, 2014
The right of Jason Page and Adrian Reynolds to be identified as the
author and illustrator of this work has been asserted in accordance
with the Copyright, Designs and Patents Act 1988.

Red Fox Books are published by Random House Children's Publishers UK,
61–63 Uxbridge Road, London W5 5SA

www.randomhousechildrens.co.uk
www.randomhouse.co.uk

Addresses for companies within The Random House Group Limited can be found at:
www.randomhouse.co.uk/offices.htm
THE RANDOM HOUSE GROUP Limited Reg. No. 954009
A CIP catalogue record for this book is available from the British Library.
Printed in China

There are **two** things you need to know about Cynthia.

The first is that she **LOVED** Christmas.

February — finish
Christmas shopping
March — send out
Christmas cards
April — wrap presents
(only 268 days to go!)
May — decorate
Christmas tree
...start
...king Christmas
dinner

It was positively her **favourite** time of year. She started looking forward to it every January. And she got **more** and **more** excited with each day that went by.

The **second** thing you need to know is that Cynthia . . .

was a **sheep.**

And the third thing (Sorry! Never was any good at maths!) is that Cynthia's flock-mates were getting a bit fed up with the constant Christmas kerfuffle.

Her pals just couldn't take any more. So they came up with a cunning plan.

"Cynthia, could I have a word?" asked Reg the Ram politely. "And a very merry Christmas to you too, Reggie!" Cynthia replied. "Fancy a snowball fight?" she added hopefully.

"Errr, not right now," said Reg. "I think I'll wait until it actually snows. The thing is, Cynthia, we've got you a present. I know it's a bit early but . . . **Happy Christmas!**"

Cynthia was delighted. Quick as a flash she ripped open the wrapping paper. Inside was a plane ticket to the North Pole . . .

". . . where Father Christmas lives!" squealed Cynthia with joy. "We thought you might like to meet him," Reg explained. "Maybe you could even lend Santa a hand. Stay as long as you like." He beamed.

Cynthia could not wait. No, really . . . she could not wait.

In half an hour she was at the airport clutching her suitcase and passport. By tea time . . .

. . . she was standing outside the entrance to Santa's Grotto. And by one minute past tea time . . .

. . . she was sitting with Father Christmas in his study drinking a nice hot chocolate.

"It's lovely to meet you," said Father Christmas cautiously. "The thing is, there's not really that much work for a sheep around here. I mean, what with all the elves, Christmas fairies and reindeer, I don't really need any more help."

Cynthia was heartbroken. "But I want to be a Little Helper.
It's what I've always dreamed of . . ." she whispered sheepishly.
Father Christmas sighed. "Well, I suppose we could try." He smiled
kindly. "Why don't we start you off in the Wrapping Room?"

"Brrrr . . . it's freezing in here," grumbled one of the elves in the Wrapping Room. But in spite of the cold his fingers and thumbs moved with lightning speed, expertly snipping, sticking, tying and folding sheets of coloured paper, ribbons and bows.

And from the blinding blur of frenzied fingers emerged the
most beautifully wrapped presents Cynthia had ever seen.
"Right!" said Cynthia. "Where do I start?"

Sadly sheep aren't great when it comes to wrapping pressies.
It might be something to do with the hooves.

"Errr . . . why don't you try the kitchens?" suggested the elf tactfully.

"Brrrrrrrr . . . it's freezing in here," shivered the cook.
"I wish Father Christmas would turn the heating up."
"Hello," said Cynthia hopefully. "I was wondering if you
needed any help."

Cook shook her head. "Sorry, dear . . . no livestock allowed in
the kitchens." She pointed to a long list of regulations pinned
to the wall. "Rules is rules. Why don't you go to the stables
and ask the reindeer?"

"Brrrrrrrr . . . it's freezing in here," said a reindeer, his teeth chattering. "No wonder my nose is red!"

Cynthia cleared her throat. "Hello. I don't suppose you need any help, do you?" she asked hopefully.
"Where are your antlers?" the reindeer asked.
"I haven't got any antlers," Cynthia said. "I'm a sheep. Sheep don't have antlers."

"Well, have a go at pulling that sleigh," said the reindeer.
At last! Cynthia had found a job!

Cynthia got into position, placed the harness
over her shoulders and pulled.
And pulled.

And PUUULLLLED.

The sleigh didn't budge. Not even an inch.
Cynthia pulled with all her might, but it was no use.

"Not as easy as it looks, is it?" said the reindeer with a shrug. "It's the antlers, you see. They make all the difference." A very disappointed Cynthia stomped out of the stable.

"It's hopeless," she cried. "No one needs my help. I'll never be a Little Helper. I might as well go home." She picked up her suitcase and headed for the door.

But Cynthia didn't get far. Suddenly in rushed a little fairy. "It's completely ruined," she wailed. "And he can't go out without it. We'll have to cancel Christmas!"

Everyone rushed into Santa's Grotto. There was Father Christmas sitting, his head in his hands. A strange whiff of burning hung in the air.

Santa was muttering: "It all happened so quickly . . . I leaned too close to the candle . . . and suddenly it was gone . . . in a puff of smoke!"
"What is it, Father Christmas?" asked Cynthia anxiously.
"What on earth is the matter?"

Father Christmas turned round and everyone **gasped**.

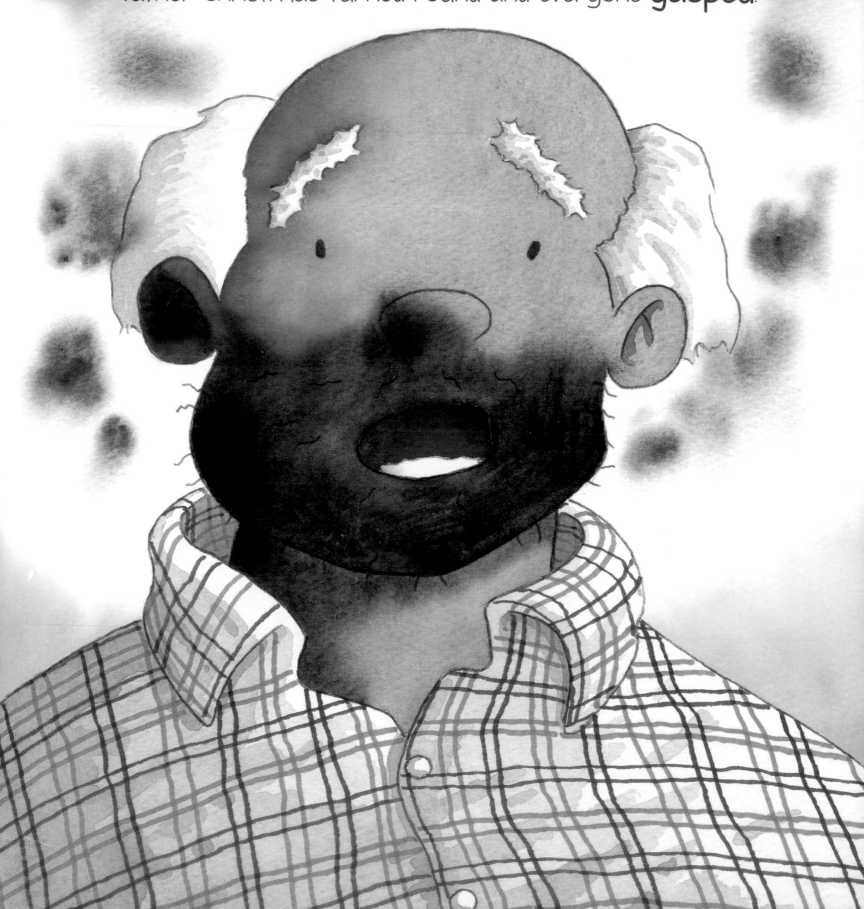

"Crikey . . . that's bad," said the elf.

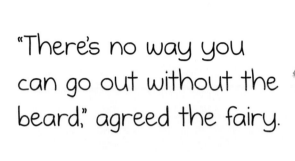

"There's no way you can go out without the beard," agreed the fairy.

"People won't recognize you," said the cook.

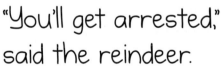

"You'll get arrested," said the reindeer.

"You're right," sighed Santa sadly, stroking the few remaining tufts of singed stubble on his now almost hairless chin. "I look ridiculous. There's nothing else for it . . .
I'm going to cancel Christmas."

"WHAT!" piped up a familiar voice.
"CANCEL CHRISTMAS? NOT ON YOUR NELLY!"

Everyone turned and stared at Cynthia. "What choice do we have?" asked the elf. "We can't send him out delivering presents looking like that. He'll get frostbite on his chin and terrify all the children." "And the grown-ups," added the reindeer.

"Don't worry, everyone - I have a plan," said Cynthia with a smile.
"Santa, come with me to your study - and bring those scissors!"
For ten minutes the sound of furious snipping filled the grotto.

Santa's Study

Finally they were done. The door opened.
And for the second time that day everyone gasped!

"Cynthia - you've saved the day!" beamed Father Christmas.
"We don't have to cancel Christmas after all . . . Cynthia?"
Everyone looked around. Where was she?
Then they heard the sound of sheepy teeth chattering.

"BRRRR . . . it's freezing in here!"

"Don't worry, Cynthia . . . it's Christmas, remember!
And look what Santa's got for you . . ."

"What do you get if you cross a sheep with a kangaroo?

. . . a lovely woolly jumper!"